Daddy and I

Written by

Lou Treleaven

Illustrated by

Sophie Burrows

For Chris - L.T

For India & Edie, whose adventures with

their ~~daddy~~ ~~ng~~ - S.B

Saturday's Daddy day, just for us two.

Making and baking - so much we can do.

But I see fields and a big blue sky.

We're off for a walk now, my Daddy and I.

We go down the lane. There are more and more trees,
And Dad finds a puddle right up to his knees.

But I see a swamp and a crocodile's eye.
We're jungle explorers, my Daddy and I.

We come to the field where the tall grass grows.

It goes past my shoulders and tickles my nose.

I lie on my belly and Dad walks right by.

We're slithering grass snakes, my Daddy and I.

We race up the hill all the way to the top,

And Dad's knee is dodgy so he has to stop.

I'll get him to do it though, just watch me try.

We're climbing a mountain, my Daddy and I.

We lie on our backs and stare into the blue,
And Dad sees a cloud like an Escort Mark Two.

But I see a shark with a giant bow tie.
We're good at cloud watching, my Daddy and I.

We go to the stream and I look for my stick.
A leaf for a sail, and we drop them in. "Quick!"
"Come ON!" we yell out as we wave them goodbye.
We're racing our sailboats, my Daddy and I.

We reach the great tree that's the oldest of all,
And Dad says it must be a hundred feet tall.
And I feel so small when I look up so high.
We're ants in this forest, my Daddy and I.

A squirrel bounds past and I want it to play,
But Daddy says hush or we'll scare it away.

I hide in the bushes and watch like a spy.
We're top secret agents, my Daddy and I.

Then suddenly – boom! – there's a terrible crack.
The sky's going dark. It's a monster attack!
But Dad says it's only a storm passing by.
We'll have to go back now, my Daddy and I.

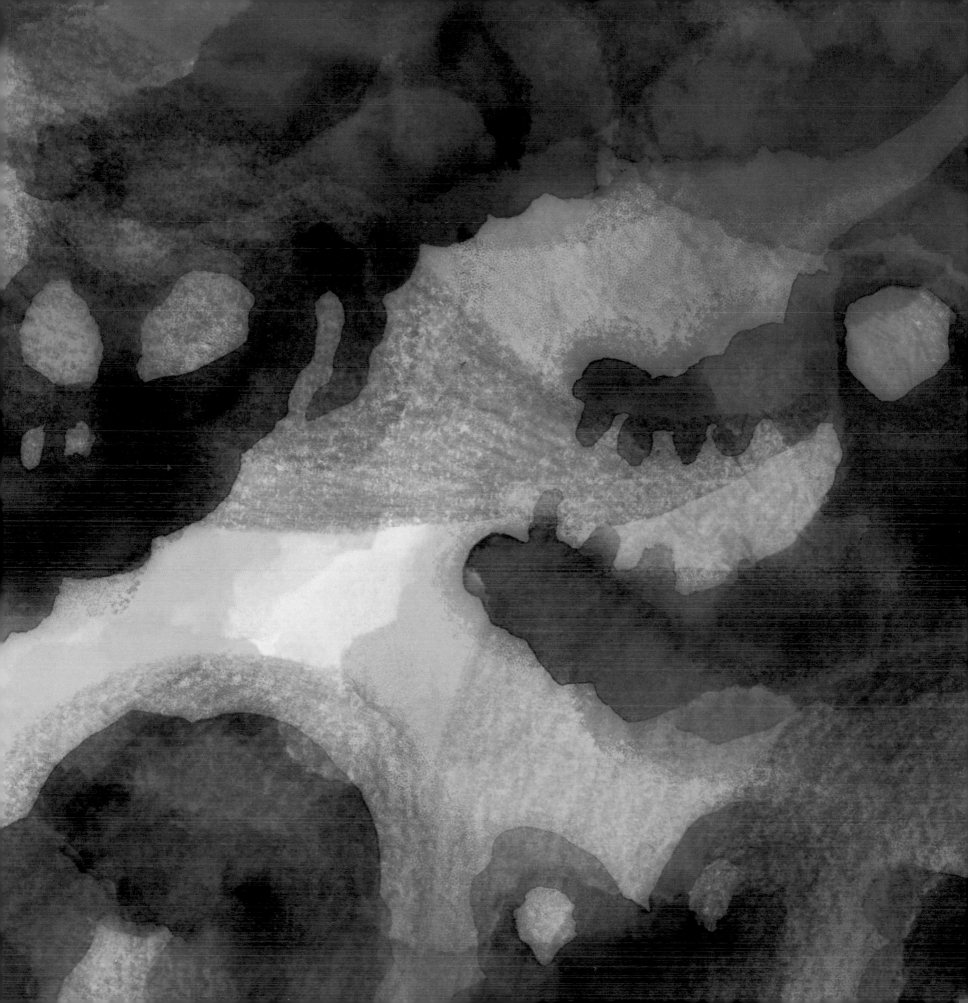

And Daddy says faster so faster we run,
But I need three steps where he only needs one.

I ride on his shoulders and now we can fly.
We zoom in our jet plane, my Daddy and I.

Then Dad puts me down and unlocks the back door.
We drip on the mat and we drip on the floor.
I wave to a whale as Dad rubs my hair dry.
We're brave deep sea-divers, my Daddy and I.

He sits by the fire, I sit on his knee,
And Dad drops a biscuit right into his tea.
It sinks like a stone, and we laugh till we cry.

We do love our Saturdays, Daddy and I.

Daddy and I
An original concept by author Lou Treleaven
© Lou Treleaven
Illustrated by Sophie Burrows

MAVERICK ARTS PUBLISHING LTD
Studio 3A, City Business Centre, 6 Brighton Road, Horsham, West Sussex, RH13 5BB
© Maverick Arts Publishing Limited   +44 (0)1403 256941

Published September 2017

A CIP catalogue record for this book is available at the British Library.

ISBN 978-1-84886-280-7

Maverick
arts publishing
www.maverickbooks.co.uk